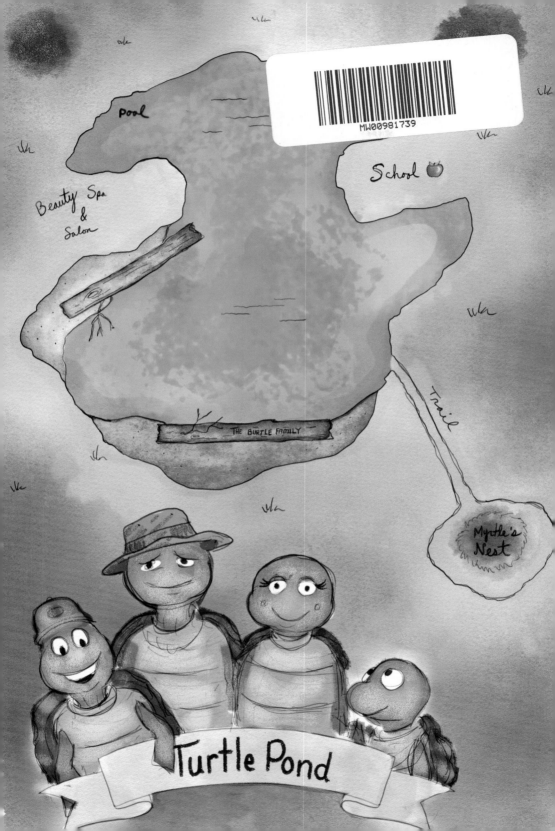

Pool

Beauty Spa & Salon

School 🍎

Trail

THE BURTLE FAMILY

Myrtle's Nest

Turtle Pond

FriesenPress

Suite 300 - 990 Fort St
Victoria, BC, Canada, V8V 3K2
www.friesenpress.com

Copyright © 2016 by Margaret Wells
First Edition — 2016

ISBN
978-1-4602-7345-6 (Paperback)
978-1-4602-7346-3 (eBook)

1. *Juvenile Fiction, Animals, Turtles*

Distributed to the trade by The Ingram Book Company

THE AMAZING ADVENTURES ON TURTLE POND

MARGARET WELLS

This book is dedicated to my wonderful grandchildren,
Brayden, Adam, Gemma, Siena and Kenzie

Margaret Wells

The Beginning of Summer

On a beautiful sunny day in May, Daddy Burtle was lying on a log in the middle of the turtle pond. He looked into the dark, murky water.

He should have felt happy. Finally, after a long winter, he could to swim to the surface of the pond and warm up on the family log.

He was so glad to see daylight at last. When he first got to the surface, he cleared his nostrils of slime from the bottom of the pond. He lay on the log for two whole days, just enjoying the warm sunshine.

But now, Mummy Myrtle was staring at him.

"You smell like warm shell!" she complained. "You can't just lie here all the time like a lump on a log!" She nudged him. "Hurtle and Squirtle are playing down below. If you go get them, I'll clean the dirt off this log, and then we can have some lunch."

With a weary "quark!"—because that's how turtles sound when they are a bit grumpy—Daddy Burtle slid off the warm log into the cool water. He dove down to the bottom of the pond to find his children.

Hurtle was excited to see his father. He started swimming around Daddy Burtle in fast circles. But he didn't look where he was going, and he accidentally bumped into his sister.

Squirtle made a noise like a wet squeak. She raced to the surface of the pond, where she squirted again and again. She just couldn't stop!

"Now look what you've done Hurtle!" said Daddy Burtle. "You know your little sister has squirting attacks when she is scared or upset. You need to be more careful. After all, you *are* the big brother..

"Sorry Dad." Said Hurtle. "I know! Why don't we collect some of those nice roots that Mom and Squirtle like to eat? We can take them to the log to eat for lunch. Maybe then they will forgive me."

Daddy Burtle thought that this was a good idea. Maybe his son wasn't quite so thoughtless after all!

By the time Daddy Burtle and Hurtle reached the log with lunch, Mummy Myrtle had calmed Squirtle. They all sat on the log, eating roots and a few bugs from the surface of the pond.

After lunch, Mummy Myrtle said, "Okay, Hurtle and Squirtle, I think it's time for a nap. You swim over to that stone under the willow trees and snooze in the shade. Burtle, you might like to visit some friends while I clean off the log again."

After everyone left, Mummy Myrtle smiled. She loved the summer on the surface of the pond. She was sure that there would be lots of adventures, and she felt it would all be okay with help from Daddy Burtle.

Humming a song, Mummy Myrtle lay down on the log to rest. Here's how her song went:

I'm Myrtle the turtle
I'm married to Burtle
We have two babies called Hurtle and Squirtle
Someday, who knows, we may have three
I'm the happiest turtle who ever could be
I'm Myrtle the turtle, that's me

Can you think of a time when you did something that upset one of your brothers or sisters?
If so, how did you make it up to them?

POND TURTLES HAVE THEIR OWN FAMILIAR LOGS THAT THEY RETURN TO EACH YEAR AFTER SLEEPING THROUGH THE WINTER AT THE BOTTOM OF THE POND.

A Scary Day for Hurtle

Hurtle was bored. He was swimming around the log in the pond. Daddy Burtle, who was trying to snooze, snapped at him to stop.

Mummy Myrtle was teaching Squirtle to relax. They were swimming along the surface of the pond and singing songs. Squirtle's song went like this:

My name is Squirtle
I'm just a wee turtle
But I'm just as happy as a turtle can be
Squirtle the turtle, that's me

Hurtle started tapping on the log with his flippers. Another of his father's glares stopped him in a hurry!

Hurtle decided to head into the pond to see if he could find anything interesting to do.

He swam towards a clump of bulrushes at the edge of the pond. Just as he got close, a duck flew off, quacking loudly.

Hurtle was so startled that he hurtled right out of the pond. He landed on his back on top of a flat rock close to the water's edge.

"Uh-oh," he thought, "now I'm in trouble!" He knew he couldn't turn over on his own. If the duck or any other big bird saw him, they would eat him for lunch.

He rocked from side to side, but that didn't help. It just made him hot under his shell. "Oh my flippers," he thought, "what am I going to do?"

Suddenly he heard a noise. It sounded like someone singing! Mummy Myrtle and Squirtle swam around a bend at the edge of the pond. He tried to make a noise, but they didn't hear him because they were singing.

Whoosh! A big bird swooped down and almost grabbed Hurtle by his under-shell. Luckily it missed, but the noise of the bird's wings made Mummy Myrtle and Squirtle look in Hurtle's direction.

Squirtle started to have a squirting attack, but Mummy Myrtle said, "Squirtle, please stop that! Hurtle needs our help. You hide under the bulrushes in case that big bird comes back."

Squirtle did as her mummy asked, making a few bubbling squirts on the way to the bulrushes. Mummy Myrtle swam to the rock that Hurtle was lying on and climbed up next to him. She pushed him with her shell until he was at the edge of the rock.

Just then, they saw the big bird's shadow and felt the air from its wings.

Squirtle also saw the big bird and couldn't help herself. She let out a loud squirt! The bird heard her and turned its head just as Mummy Myrtle pushed Hurtle off the rock and followed him into the pond.

Mummy Myrtle, Hurtle, and Squirtle swam back to the log where Daddy Burtle was sunning himself. "Did you have a good day?" he asked.

Mummy Myrtle said, "I'll tell you later. Meanwhile, could you please find us some lunch? Thank you!"

What do you do if you're bored?

Can you think of a time when someone saved you from a bad situation?

A TURTLE'S TOP SHELL IS CALLED A **CARAPACE**, AND ITS UNDERSHELL IS CALLED A **PLASTRON.**

The First Day of School

On a lovely day in May, Hurtle and Squirtle went to school.

Turtles hibernate (sleep) all winter, so young turtles have to go to school in the summer. They must learn important things like how to stay away from predators (animals that eat other animals), how to look for food, and how to watch out for one another. Watching out for one another is *very* important!

Daddy Burtle took Hurtle and Squirtle to the school, which was just a flat stone under some bulrushes. Their teacher was named Teacher Thoughtful.

She guided Squirtle to the front of the stone closest to her. She put Hurtle just behind Squirtle. There were several other young turtles in the class. Their families lived on their own logs in different parts of the pond.

The young turtle sitting next to Squirtle was a larger pond turtle. He was *twice* the size of Hurtle and *three times* the size of Squirtle. His name was Brutle Jr.

Teacher Thoughtful was explaining to the class what she was going to teach them. Suddenly Brutle Jr. gave Squirtle a big nudge.

"Hey, Squirt," he said. "How boring is this? Why don't you and I swim around for a while and find something more fun to do?"

Squirtle had been told by her parents *never* to go anywhere with strangers. She felt very frightened by this big, bold turtle. What should she do? She started to squirt!

Hurtle heard Brutle Jr. He hurtled over his seat and hit Brutle Jr. hard on the back of his shell.

Now what?

Teacher Thoughtful had taught turtles for many years. She had seen this kind of behavior before.

"Hurtle," she said, "please go back to your seat. Squirtle, are you okay?"

Squirtle gave a little squirt but nodded.

Teacher Thoughtful looked at the class and said, "As I told you earlier, watching out for one another is *very* important. However, it doesn't include hitting anyone."

"Both of you boys were wrong in what you did. You will stay behind today and help clean up the weeds around the school. Brutle Jr., please tell Squirtle that you're sorry for upsetting her."

The boys grumbled but knew that Teacher Thoughtful was right.

At the end of the day, Teacher Thoughtful felt happy that she had taught all her students a good lesson.

If someone you didn't know asked you to go somewhere with them, what would you do?

Do you think Hurtle did the right thing when he tried to help Squirtle?

HIBERNATION IS WHEN ANIMALS GO TO SLEEP FOR THE WINTER. TURTLES HIBERNATE AT THE BOTTOM OF A POND.

A **PREDATOR** IS AN ANIMAL THAT EATS OTHER ANIMALS.

Grandpa Clemmy

It was a sunny day in early June.

Daddy Burtle and Hurtle were on a fishing trip. They were looking for tadpoles and larvae (baby bugs) for lunch. They both liked to eat these rather than the bulrush roots that Mummy Myrtle and Squirtle enjoyed.

They usually started out close to the willow trees that hung over the pond and where frogs liked to lay their eggs. They would dive down and often find the frogspawn (frog eggs) attached to the grasses just under the surface of the pond. These eggs were really tasty!

On a really good trip, they would find some baby tadpoles that had just hatched from their eggs. These were more filling and an extra treat!

Meanwhile, Mummy Myrtle went to wake up Squirtle, who was napping on a flat stone under a willow tree at the edge of the pond.

Squirtle, who was just waking up, gave a big yawn then a little squirt. When she saw her mother, she smiled and reached up on her little back flippers for a hug.

Mummy Myrtle thought it was wonderful to have such a loving little girl. She hoped to have another one someday.

"Come on, sweetie," Mummy Myrtle said. "You and I are going to visit Grandpa Clemmy."

Right away the smile left Squirtle's face. "Mummy, I don't like going to visit Grandpa Clemmy. He scares me! He is so old and wrinkled, and he doesn't even know who I am!"

"Now, Squirtle," said Mummy Myrtle, "Grandpa Clemmy and Grandma Marmorata—we called her Marmy for short—were very special turtles. They brought your daddy and me to this pond many years ago so we could have a safe home.

"Poor Marmy went to turtle heaven before you were born, so Grandpa Clemmy decided to go to a turtles' retirement nest. The kind turtles there make sure he is safe and happy.

"I know he is sometimes forgetful. He can also be a bit of a grumpy grampy, but we still love him very much."

Squirtle, who is a very kind little turtle, said, "Okay, Mummy, let's go. I'll take Grandpa some bulrushes to hang in his room in the retirement nest. He can nibble their shoots if his beak is still strong enough."

"That's my girl!" said Mummy Myrtle, and off they went.

Have you ever collected frogspawn or tadpoles from a pond? What did you do with them?

Do you think Squirtle should have been afraid of Grandpa Clemmy?

A POND TURTLE'S PROPER NAME IS **CLEMMIS MARMORATA**.

LARVAE ARE BABY INSECTS THAT OFTEN LOOK LIKE WORMS.

FROGSPAWN ARE THE EGGS LAID BY FROGS FROM WHICH TADPOLES HATCH.

Mummy Myrtle's Day Out

It was a hot day in July, and Mummy Myrtle felt hot and bothered. The family had eaten breakfast, and now she was trying to clean up the log. Daddy Burtle was sleeping on one end and the children were pushing each other to see who would fall off the log first.

Suddenly Mummy Myrtle flipped out! She waved her flippers and told the children to play somewhere else in the pond.

The noise woke up Daddy Burtle. He looked at Mummy Myrtle in surprise. She was usually so sweet and patient. What could be the matter?

He went over to sit by her on the log. "What is wrong, dear?" he asked.

"Oh, I'm sorry, Burtle. It's just so hot, and I need some time to myself so that I can cool off," said Mummy Myrtle.

"Well then," said Daddy Burtle, "why don't you take the day off and go to Miss Beautle's Salon and Spa? I'll look after Hurtle and Squirtle."

"Oh, thank you, Burtle," said Mummy Myrtle. She kissed him on his beak. Daddy Burtle dove into the pond to look for his children.

Myrtle thought of her kind, thoughtful husband and sang her song:

> *I'm Myrtle the turtle*
> *I'm married to Burtle*
> *We have two babies called Hurtle and Squirtle*
> *Someday, who knows, we may have three*
> *I'm the happiest turtle who ever could be*
> *I'm Myrtle the turtle, that's me*

Then she swam off to Miss Beautle's Salon and Spa.

When she got there, some of her friends were already there. They were relaxing in a warm pool next to the salon at the edge of the pond.

They were all there for different reasons. Some of the ladies needed their beaks shaved. Others needed their claws clipped. Some were there just to enjoy a quiet day with friends.

Miss Beautle welcomed Mummy Myrtle and asked, "What can I do for you today?"

"Well," said Mummy Myrtle, "I really need my shell polished and I'd like my claws clipped and painted."

"No problem!" said Miss Beautle. "Come this way."

She took Mummy Myrtle to a flat rock above the pool and sat her down. She first asked what colour Mummy Myrtle would like her claws painted. Mummy Myrtle chose a pretty yellow to match parts of her shell.

Miss Beautle clipped and painted Mummy Myrtle's claws. Later, while she was having a nice-smelling polish rubbed onto her shell, Mummy Myrtle fell asleep. When she woke up, Miss Beautle told her to look at herself in the pond.

Mummy Myrtle couldn't believe how lovely she looked! She also felt calm and relaxed after a whole day of being taken care of.

She slipped back into the pond, said goodbye to her friends in the pool, and swam home to the family log.

When she got home, it was quite dark. Hurtle and Squirtle were playing a game with stones on the log, trying to see who could flipper the stones farthest. They looked at her with their big eyes opened wide! Was this beautiful lady their mummy? Daddy Burtle couldn't stop looking at his wife, either!

Mummy Myrtle climbed onto the log.

After the children fell asleep, Daddy Burtle and Mummy Myrtle snuggled up to do a little flirtling.

 Does your Mummy ever go to the salon?

What does she have done to make her look pretty?

Brooding

On a cool day in October, Mummy Myrtle felt restless. How had summer ended so fast?

The children were having one last lesson at Teacher Thoughtful's school. Daddy Burtle was with some friends. Mummy Myrtle was alone for once.

She sat on the family log and thought. As she began to doze, her thoughts turned into a dream. In her head she could see a baby turtle sleeping in a little warm nest.

In her dream she was singing a little lullaby to the baby:

> *I am your mummy*
> *You were in my tummy*
> *I laid some eggs early one morn*
> *After a while, you came to be born*
> *Wasn't I clever?*
> *I'll love you for ever!*

Later in the day, Daddy Burtle and the children came back to the log. After a supper of bulrush roots and bugs, Mummy Myrtle sat on the end of the log. She was humming the lullaby to herself.

The sun went down over the pond. The moon came up. Daddy Burtle, Hurtle, and Squirtle went down to their nest for the night.

Mummy Myrtle slipped quietly off the log into the cool, dark pond. She swam to the bank, climbed out, and started to walk. Where was she going?

She walked a long time because it is hard for pond turtles to move quickly on land. Finally, she found the place she was looking for. She scooped out a hole in the soft sand with her flippers and laid her eggs. Then she covered them with sand to keep them warm until they hatched. Very slowly, she made her way back to the pond.

When Hurtle and Squirtle woke up the next day, Mummy Myrtle was nowhere to be seen! Where was she? Mummy was always there to look after them!

Daddy Burtle knew that this had happened twice before: once before Hurtle was born and once before Squirtle was born. He smiled and got breakfast for Hurtle and Squirtle. "Mummy will be back soon," he said. "Don't worry."

The day passed, and it was supper-time. Suddenly, Mummy Myrtle arrived at the log, looking very tired. Daddy Burtle helped her up onto the log and kissed her beak.

"Children," he said, "please don't bother your mummy with anything right now. She's very tired. Tomorrow she will be fine."

Do you think that in the spring, there will be another little turtle to share the family log?

What name would you give it?

FEMALE TURTLES WALK A LONG WAY INLAND TO LAY THEIR EGGS. THEY COVER THEM WITH SAND OR SOIL TO KEEP THEM WARM. THE BABIES HATCH AFTER TWO OR THREE MONTHS, AND THEIR MUMMY GOES BACK TO GET THEM IN THE SPRING.

ONLY ONE OR TWO BABIES MAKE IT BACK TO THE POND BECAUSE OF **PREDATORS**. DO YOU REMEMBER WHAT A **PREDATOR** IS?

HATCHING IS WHEN BABY ANIMALS AND BIRDS BREAK OUT OF THEIR EGGS.

Stormy Weather

It was an early day in November. Clouds were flying over the pond. Suddenly the clouds opened, and the rain fell in huge drops. The wind roared and roared.

The turtles hid in their nests under the surface of the pond. They were scared that they would be washed away.

Daddy Burtle held Hurtle in *his* flippers, and Mummy Myrtle held Squirtle in *her* flippers.

They all huddled together and listened to the thunder roaring and the rain pouring down on the pond.

Hurtle was trying to be brave, but he was shaking in his shell. Every now and again, Squirtle gave a little squirt.

Mummy Myrtle was worried about Grandpa Clemmy in the retirement nest way down below in the pond. Was he okay she wondered?

She also worried about the eggs she had laid and buried on land. She thought she had walked far enough away from the water's edge so that they would be safe, but she wasn't quite sure.

Suddenly there was a *huge* crash. A tree had fallen into the pond, creating a *gigantic* wave.

Daddy Burtle and Mummy Myrtle were thrown out of their nests and into different parts of the pond. Daddy Burtle held onto Hurtle with his strong flippers. But Mummy Myrtle wasn't strong enough to hold onto Squirtle. Squirtle was thrown out of her mummy's flippers into the darkness of the storm.

In the darkness the Burtle family could hear the quarks of other turtles who were also clinging to one another in the storm.

At last the storm was over. There was an eerie hush over the pond. The rain stopped, the clouds went away, and a strange, watery sun shone.

Daddy Burtle came out of the pond with Hurtle still in his flippers. They blew out mud and dirt from their eyes and nostrils.

Now it was time to get the family back together! Daddy Burtle spotted Mummy Myrtle clinging to their log. Yes! Their log had made it through the storm. But something was wrong. Where was Squirtle?

Mummy Myrtle was very worried for her little daughter. She felt guilty that she couldn't hang on to her. Daddy Burtle said it wasn't her fault. She had done the best that any turtle could do!

Suddenly there was a low whistle from Hurtle. He was calling his pals all over the pond. Soon the hunt for Squirtle was on! With so many turtles helping, it was easier to look in more places.

Everyone swam around the pond to search for Squirtle. They looked under the surface of the pond to see if she was in a nest somewhere. They looked under bulrushes and stones around the edge of the pond.

All of a sudden, there was a burst of water from the bottom of the pond. Squirtle catapulted out of the water, followed by Grandpa Clemmy.

Squirtle had landed in the retirement nest which had not been damaged by the storm. After the storm was over, Grandpa Clemmy pushed her up to the surface of the pond.

Everyone shouted with joy!

Mummy Myrtle rushed over, held Squirtle in her flippers, and kissed her little beak. "Oh, how I love you," Mummy Myrtle said.

"And I love you, too, Mummy," said Squirtle, happy to be in her mother's safe flippers.

Daddy Burtle went to Grandpa Clemmy and clapped him on his shell. "Well done, Clemmy," he said. "Thank you so much. You are wiser than people think."

Grandpa Clemmy blushed and gave a "quark" but winked at Daddy Burtle before he went back to the retirement nest.

Turning to Hurtle, Daddy Burtle said, "Hurtle, you have a group of friends who are very loyal to you. That means that you treat them nicely and you all have similar values. I'm proud of you, son."

Hurtle blushed under his shell but felt very happy that his father saw him as a responsible turtle and not just a hurtling hooligan.

How things had changed over the summer! The Burtle family was still together on the family log and had grown to know and respect one another better.

Have you ever experienced a big storm?
Were you afraid?

TO CATAPULT MEANS THAT SOMETHING OR SOMEBODY
IS FLUNG INTO THE AIR WITH GREAT SPEED.

The Talent Show

It was the end of the school year. To celebrate, Teacher Thoughtful put together a talent show. All of her students were going to perform.

Hurtle and Squirtle were very excited, but they didn't know what they could do.

"Well, Hurtle," said Mummy Myrtle, "maybe you could do some of that wonderful hip hop dancing that you do on your back flippers. I've seen you do some great hurtling moves here on the pond."

Daddy Burtle looked at Squirtle and said, "You know, sweetie, you could squirt the school song. You have a lovely squirting voice."

Hurtle and Squirtle were encouraged by what their parents said and started practicing right away!

On another log in the pond, Brutle Jr. decided that he would show how strong he was in the talent show. He practiced lifting logs until his front flippers became *huge*. He was sure he was going to be the best turtle in the show.

Finally the day of the talent show came!

All the students and their parents were on the school stone at the edge of the pond. Teacher Thoughtful was dressed in her teacher's robes and looked very proud of her students.

One by one, the young turtles performed the talents they had been practicing. One group of girl turtles did some synchronized swimming. They glided around the pond and fanned out their flippers to make beautiful patterns in the water.

When it was time for Hurtle to do his dance, he stood on the flat rock by the edge of the pond and waited for the music. The music came from frogs, dragonflies, and bugs croaking and buzzing.

Hurtle got up on his back flippers and took off, twirling, hopping, somersaulting, and finally ending with a back flip into the pond.

Everyone went wild! They clapped until Hurtle climbed back onto the stone stage, bowed, and went back to be with the other students.

Now it was time for Brutle Jr. to perform. He went to the front of the stone stage and showed off his muscles. Then he picked up the log that two other large turtles had brought onto the stage for him.

With a grunt, he lifted the huge log and held it above his head. Everyone gasped in wonder. Brutle Jr. was thinking that he was the best turtle in the show when the log slipped from his flippers. It knocked him backwards onto his carapace and landed across his front flippers. He couldn't move!

The audience let out a scared gasp.

Suddenly there was a low whistle, and Hurtle and his friends gathered around Brutle Jr. With a lot of grunting, they lifted the log off Brutle Jr's flippers. They turned him the right way up and patted his shell to get him breathing again.

Everyone roared with happiness. Hurtle and his friends had saved the day!

Brutle Jr., still looking a little shaky, crawled over to Hurtle. "Thank you, my friend," he croaked. "You will never have to fear my family and me again." He gave Hurtle a high-five flipper and crept away.

After all the excitement, Teacher Thoughtful said it was time for Squirtle to end the show by squirting the school song.

Squirtle looked nervous, but a smile from Mummy Myrtle gave her the courage she needed. She sang:

Hurrah for Teacher Thoughtful!
She's taught us all we know
How to be good turtles
And how to learn and grow

Let's show her how we love her
And thank her for her worth
With lots of love and laughter
So squirt, squirt, squirt, squirt, squirt

With a final squirt, Squirtle plopped down on the stone stage.

Teacher Thoughtful lifted up Squirtle and hugged her.

"What a wonderful way to end the school year," she said. "I look forward to seeing you and Hurtle in class next year. You have been good examples and excellent students!"

Everyone thought that the talent show had been a huge success.

Daddy Burtle and Mummy Myrtle felt very proud of Hurtle and Squirtle. They all swam back to their log. Then they had a supper of bugs and bulrush roots before sliding into their nest for the night and for the winter.

Night-night, turtles. Sleep well. See you in the spring!

Do you remember what a CARAPACE is?

A SOMERSAULT IS WHEN SOMEONE TURNS HEAD OVER HEELS IN THE AIR AND LANDS ON THEIR FEET.

SYNCHRONIZED MEANS WHEN TWO OR MORE PEOPLE DO THE SAME THING AT THE SAME TIME.

Printed in Canada